P9-DBX-941

SCHOOL PROGRAM
REET
BRIGHTON, MA 02135

INSIDE OUTSIDE UPSIDE DOWN

INSIDE OUTSIDE UPSIDE DOWN

by Stan and Jan Berenstain

A Bright & Early Book
RANDOM HOUSE/NEW YORK

Copyright © 1968 by Stanley and Janice Berenstain. All rights reserved under International and Pan-American Copyright Conventions. Published in the United States by Random House, Inc., New York, and simultaneously in Canada by Random House of Canada Limited, Toronto. Library of Congress Catalog Card Number: 68-28465. Manufactured in the United States of America.

L M N O

56

Going in

Inside

Inside a box

Upside down

Inside a box
Upside down

Going out

Outside

THIS
SIDE
UP

Outside
Inside a box
Upside down

THIS SIDE UP

Going on

On a truck
Outside
Inside a box
Upside down

Going

Going to town
On a truck
Outside
Inside a box
Upside down

Falling off

Off the truck

Coming out

Right side up!

Mama! Mama!
I went to town.
Inside,
Outside,
Upside down!